THE START OF NOTHING

the inevitable series book one

L.M. RICHARDSON

This book is
brought to you by

ISBN: 9798730981751

Cover designed by Mercy B. Carruthers

*This book is dedicated to young love, and friends
who find themselves wanting more than a friendship.*

CHAPTER ONE

"Ooo, don't look now, but here comes Nandi's boyfriend, *mister come be my hero*. He's coming to get her books and walk her to his car," Emily interrupted Amber in the middle of her daily after school meltdown about how much homework she has, or whatever the crisis of the day is.

"He is not my boyfriend," I snapped.

"Does he know that? I'm just saying," Emily smiled, waving him over like an animated fool, and the rest of the girls follow suit waving and laughing like idiots.

"I've told y'all a thousand times, Heero is not my boyfriend. And yes, he knows that. We're just... Why am I even explaining myself? But I'm going to say it one last time. We are just friends," I said wondering to myself if we are in fact friends, acquaintances, or buddies.

"With friends like Heero, you don't need a boyfriend Nandi," Amber stopped complaining for two seconds to cosign Emily's nonsense. "Girl he's so fine. And he's a perfect gentleman."

"Any guy who sniffs you out wherever you are, greets you with a hug, takes your backpack and walks you to his car to take you to wherever the two of you go when you leave school is definitely a boyfriend in my book," Pixie joined the conversation.

"Not you too, Pix. Again, we are training together for this upcoming marathon. He's running the full, and I'm walking the 5K. And on the days I have physical therapy, he drops me off, because my dad can't leave work to get me there after school. Besides, he's not my type," I explain for the umpteenth time.

"Nandi, you're too smart to be this dumb. Heero is not doing all of this do-gooder boy schout crap because he just wants to see you get back to basketball. Or whatever it is you tell yourself to deny that you have feelings for him. Look at him. It's written all over the smile on his face when he looks at you. And in the stride in his walk to get to you. Heero is definitely your boyfriend. Whether you're his girlfriend is another story."

"Since you don't want him, I'll take mister just *my* type off your hands." Emily flirtatiously waved at him again, as he finally makes it to us.

"Heeey, Heero," the two of them purr in unison. They are sick.

"Hey ladies," Heero nervously laughs at their antics and takes my backpack off my shoulders. "Sorry ladies. Do you mind if I steal Nandi from you?"

"If she doesn't want to go with you, I will," Emily bats her eyes.

"Bye already. I'll talk to y'all later." I turn and walk away with Heero.

Emily is my best friend. We've been friends since we were five years old, playing basketball on the same team at the youth center. During a game, I got kicked in the foot, and fell screaming. Emily ran to me and took over. "My parents are doctors, and I will be too one day. Let me take a look at your foot," she said. And she's been taking care of my cuts, scrapes, and cramps, as well as offering unsolicited medical advice ever since.

At the end of third grade her family moved away for two years, when her parents were running a clinic in an underserved rural area. The entire time we wrote each other and kept in touch. They returned to

Caledonia to open a clinic in The Bottoms, and we picked up like we were never separated. Our parents made sure we were always on the same teams for youth basketball. And when I tore my ACL, Emily was the first to get to me, before the coach could make it off the bench, or my dad out of the stands. She held my hand and was my nurse before and after surgery. She's more than a best friend, she's the sister that I never had.

Amber and Pixie complete our sister circle. We met them in junior high school, where we played basketball together at Milton Crenshaw Junior High. We're tighter than panty hose three sizes too small.

"Why are you looking at me like that?" Heero questions.

"What? I'm not looking at you," I suck my teeth.

"You were definitely studying me."

"If you're driving, with your eyes on the road, how could you tell if I was looking at you? Which I was absolutely not studying you. Wishful thinking," I continued to plead my case.

"Why can't you admit that you were studying me, and you like what you see?"

"Okay," I take a deep breath, "I was… not looking at you, Heero."

We both laugh. I cut my eye at him to make sure

he is not watching. I was looking at Heero, and I was caught, but I couldn't tell him that I was trying to figure him out. After my conversation with the girls, it has me wondering, *does he like me like that*? And the bigger question, *do I like him*?

"What's the matter? You seem distracted today," Yoshi, my physical therapist asks. "Listen, it's really important that you stay focused. I need you to give me everything you've got, then dig deep and give me some more. We only have a few more sessions and if I'm going to clear you, you have to hit several more benchmarks."

"I'm focused. Really. I am focused." I put my game face on, trying to convince Yoshi that I'm all in. In the few months we've known each other, he's been able to read me like a book. I am distracted, and more than a little bit. Emily and the girls are all up in my head. *Focus. Focus. Focus.*

"Nandi, second guessing yourself and being distracted can result in injury. I know you get tired of me pushing but it's my job to give you the tools you need to get you back on your feet and stronger than before. Do the exercises like I showed you, with confidence and accuracy. There are no short cuts to excellence." Yoshi is not shy about calling his patients out and putting them in their place.

"Okay, I get it. I understand."

"And that goes for more than physical therapy, that includes life as well. I see you, Nandi. You're very smart, my mom would say you have a lot of book sense. Everything is not by the book with set schedules, timetables, and outcomes. There are some things you have to experience for yourself, sitting on the sidelines and watching it happen to others will get you nowhere. Don't be afraid to wade into the deep end, the water is fine." Yoshi was eyeing Heero sitting in the waiting area doing his homework.

"Obviously you're not just talking about my knee and recovery. And I am totally confused right now. The deep end, water, what?" I laugh and make light of what he said, but I understand clearly what Yoshi means.

When I started physical therapy, I was supposed to be with Kate, the other therapist in the office with Yoshi, but another parent told my dad we should ask for Yoshi. There have been days that I didn't like him very much. He pushes me further than I wanted to go more than a few times. Once, I kept scooting away from him, until I almost scooted right off the two-foot therapy table onto my head.

Yoshi was off a few times and I had to work with Kate. I thought since they work together, she would provide the same level of therapy. Not at all. She is much more laxed than he is. She asked if I felt up to an exercise. When I told her no, she didn't push back, instead she gave me something easier and we ended my session early. Yoshi would never. Had Kate been my regular therapist, I would still be walking with a limp. I'm thankful for Yoshi pushing me to be better.

"Earth to Nandi. We're finally done for the day. You're free to leave with your boyfriend." Yoshi snapped his fingers in my face. "And don't put your brace back on today, it's time to start going without it more often. Get comfortable with not having to use it."

"He's not my… never mind." I rolled my eyes and walked past Heero as if I didn't see him sitting there waiting for me.

CHAPTER TWO

"You've got to be kidding me. You're stopping again to adjust your brace," Heero fussed making his way back to me. "This is what, the third time in fifteen minutes, Nandi? When are you planning to stop wearing that thing? It's falling apart, the screws keep backing out, and you're carrying around a screwdriver to fix it. You're bum brace is slowing down our training," Heero fussed after I stopped again to adjust my brace.

"Just give me a second. You don't have to be such a cry baby," I said patting my pants realizing my screwdriver was in the car and not in my pocket.

"Both your doctor and physical therapist said you don't need it anymore. Come on Nandi, at this point you're just using it as a crutch. Do us both a favor and throw it away. There's a dumpster over there. Let me do the honors."

"You're being such a pain right now. I don't *need* my brace, I *want* it. And maybe it is a crutch, maybe it's not. You don't know everything. What the doctor *and* physical therapist said is, I can put it away when I'm ready. And today is not that day. I am not ready. Don't let me hold you up from your training."

"I didn't mean… what I meant to say is, I've been there, after my Achilles injury," Heero tried to explain.

"Yeah, yeah. You've told me a million times about your injury. And I know exactly what you meant. Your injury ain't nothing like mine. Okay? And I don't have to get rid of my brace because you got rid of yours. Leave me alone!"

"Wait. Where are you going? Nandi wait up," Heero came running behind me.

"Hold up for what? Don't let me keep you up from your training. Go ahead and finish your run. I'm going back to the car to put the screw back in my brace." I turned around and walked away from Heero, refusing to turn around to see if he was still there. Finally, I hear him running away.

"You're impossible!" Heero yells.

In the third basketball game of my senior season, I

tore my ACL in a game against our archrivals. It was the fourth quarter, and I was having an amazing game. Everything I put up went in. I was like Flash, all over the court stealing, rebounding, and assisting. The best part was a coach from one of my top three schools was in the stands.

I stole the ball and made a fast break for the basket. I went up for a layup, it went in, of course. Coming down, someone ran under me and I came down awkward. Not only did I hear the pop in my knee, but I felt it all over my body. The pain was more intense than I've ever felt in my life, and the scream I let out signified such. Immediately, I knew it was all over. My senior season was gone before it got started.

Coach Pratt, the trainer, and my dad all tried to make me feel better and encourage me to think positive. "We'll wait to see what the doctor says. It may be a sprain or hyperextension," Coach said.

This season was supposed to be the icing on the cake to an extraordinary high school basketball career, the best f'ing year ever. It turned out to be anything but. From the injury to surgery and physical therapy. I've struggled with it all. As soon as I was no longer the star basketball player, my boyfriend, Preston, moved on to the next, even before I was able to come back to school after my surgery.

What hurt the most is all the colleges that were recruiting me pre-injury stopped calling and texting. All communication ceased. The letters, calls, and visits started after my sophomore season. I was getting mail from schools in every division. When they stopped reaching out to me, I was devastated, felt betrayed and isolated. I was more hurt about the end of being recruited than Preston dumping me. All I did was eat and sleep. It wasn't long before the pounds started adding up. In just a few months, I was ten pounds heavier, not able to fit in my clothes and was stuck wearing sweats that could fit over my brace.

The two things I've been able to count on outside of my Dad, Gigi, and occasionally Herro has been food and my brace. The metal contraption has been my support since the surgery. I've done nothing without it. It's been the first thing I reach for in the morning, and the last thing at night, and now it's giving out on me too.

I've always had dreams of playing for a division one college program, far away from home. One that would allow me the opportunity to play on TV. In the process, making my dad proud, the payoff for all of his time and effort. And for my mom to see me and realize what she's missed out on.

Daddy has coached me in basketball since I was a little girl. Gigi said, for my first birthday, he bought me a doll and basketball that matched his. I carried the doll in one hand, and the basketball under my other arm. Eventually, I chose the basketball over the doll. We'd dribble in the house driving everyone else around us crazy. I've always had a basketball goal in my bedroom, and several balls for it. Mama hid balls, so I wouldn't throw them against the wall trying to make the basket. Daddy bought more.

It's been five months since my injury and surgery, and physical therapy started the week after surgery. According to Yoshi, I'm doing great, but physical therapy alone isn't enough if I'm going to get back to basketball. My range of motion is almost where it should be, I'm able to walk without limping and my knee is strong enough to support regular physical activity. The key words are strong enough, support and without limping. But I'm not ready to play basketball yet.

Yoshi suggested sports rehabilitation, but we can't afford it. It's just me and Daddy. He works hard to provide for me by himself. He has a good job with Murphy Construction but helping out Gigi and Papa after my mom left, and more so now that Papa has been sick, Daddy stresses sometimes about how to make ends meet, and I don't want to add to it. Coach Pratt knows how important basketball is to me and having an athletic scholarship in addition to academics is the only way I'm going to be able to pay for college. He suggested I work out with Heero, train for the Caledonia Marathon, and compete in the 5K.

A couple of years ago in tenth grade, Heero suffered a devastating Achilles injury while playing football. Like me, he went through a surgery and physical therapy. While in sports rehab to get back to football the following year, he started running, working his way up from running one mile to three. Then from three miles to five. One day he was out running, ran into a group and ran with them. They were a running club and were training for a marathon. Heero ran with them every chance he could, and one thing led to another. He signed up for his first 10K, and gradually made his way to half marathons. Heero has run races all over the state and has an arm full of medals to show for it. Since his injury Heero hasn't gone back to football. He says he doesn't love it like he used to. That passion has been replaced by running, and this year he's running his very first marathon.

Here we are, Heero and I are preparing for the Caledonia Marathon in June. I'm race walking the 5K and Heero is competing in the full marathon, twenty-six point two miles. He's ran six half marathons before, and this will be his first full marathon. Heero is more than serious about this marathon and training. He eats, drinks, and sleeps for the marathon and it's all he talks about.

Coach thinks I still have a shot at playing D1 basketball. The days I'm not running with Heero, I'm in the basketball gym. He says between the two, I'll rebuild my confidence, and endurance, putting me in a great position. "Coaches like a good comeback story. And you're going to give them one," he says.

I might have to walk-on my freshman year, but with my grades I should be able to secure enough scholarships to pay for school. Coach has always been in my corner. The morning of my surgery when we walked into the hospital to check in at six a.m., he was already there waiting for us. Daddy said he wouldn't leave until I was out of surgery. I'd like to think I'm special, but I know he will do the same for all of his players.

Of all the schools that were recruiting me, only one continues to have contact, Holly Springs Prep, a junior college. Coach knows the head coach, they played college basketball together. It's closer to home than I want to be. "It's a good school, and you can get a quality education, getting you ready for the next level. After all, education and a sustainable career are the goals, not the WNBA," Coach reminds me often.

A four-year university is my goal, and I'm not interested in anything less. Coach and my counselor both say I should keep my options open. But I know what I want, and I'm sticking to my guns.

By the time I finally get the screw back in place, I see Heero in the distance running toward the car where I'm sitting on the hood. His form is perfect, and his pace rhythmic, as if he were running to music. He doesn't like listening to music when he runs. "I run to the beat of my heart," he told me when I first asked about his running playlist. At first, I thought he was just being sarcastic. I wanted to laugh, but quickly realized he was dead serious. And it makes it even more amazing to watch. Heero's entire body is in sync, one fluid motion.

Without saying a word, Heero got in and started the car. Still fidgeting with my brace, I catch him rolling his eyes and sucking his teeth. I take my time getting in, and before I can close the door, he snatches the car into reverse and starts backing up. Clearly, he's upset, and I kept all comments to myself just in case.

"What are your expectations?" Heero finally speaks.

"Excuse me?" I have no idea what he is talking about.

"Your expectations. Are you working out and training with an end goal in mind, or just going through the motions for the fun of it? I mean if you're only in it for the fun that's okay too. There is something I need you to know. I'm serious about my training, it's not something I'm doing to pass the time, and I don't have time to waste. When we started working out together, I thought we were on the same page. But today I'm not so sure. Doing something you've never done, or to obtain a goal you've never reached you have to take a few risks. Do you understand what I'm saying?"

"Risks huh?" I mock. "What risks are you taking? Training with me and spending so much time with a girl that's not from your social circles. Oh, I know. I know that your mom thinks I'm some pity case, and I'm not worth your time, because I'm not a debutante. Heero you already have your path paved for you. And you're being groomed to step into your parents' footsteps. You will go to the university your brothers, mom, dad, and grandfather attended. You don't have to worry about scholarships, grants, financial aid, or how you'll pay for college. Dude, you have a college fund, trust fund and connections. And once you get to those hallowed halls, you'll study law just like all of your family has, then step right into the family business. None of that is an option for me.

"I have good grades and always have, but it is not enough. I'll still need an athletic scholarship. My dad has raised me by himself, and although he does okay, he has more than me to think about. He also helps Gigi take care of bills for Pops because insurance won't pay for all the care he needs. I don't have a college fund, trust fund or any other fund. I have to figure it out. So yeah, I do have expectations and goals in mind. I expect to strengthen my leg, continue to work out and hopefully get another shot at impressing the division one schools who were once interested in me. The scholarships might be all gone, but I still plan to play. I'm sorry if me holding on to my raggedy brace bothers you so much. Right now, it gives me peace of mind, even though it's falling apart. You might not understand it, but like Linus and his blanket, I need this brace right now."

I turned around in my seat and don't say another word.

"We good for tomorrow?" Heero asks, in a softer gentler tone when he pulls up in front of my house. He flashed a smile showing all of his perfectly aligned teeth, thanks to three years of braces.

"Yes, we're good for tomorrow," I returned his smile and open the door.

"Nandi wait." Heero caught my hand, and I turn to see the sincerest look on his face. "I do have great big shoes to fill. Living in the shadows of my older brothers, parents and grandfather isn't easy. And trying to live up to their expectations scares me and drives me at the same time. I'm not half as smart as you, and I have to work twice as hard to maintain a B minus average. Running is something I'm good at without trying, and it's all mine. It's not anything my family has done or excels in, and they actually praise me for it. I apologize for being an ass."

"Apology accepted, your assness."

"Thanks."

"My hand. You have to let go of my hand if I'm going to get out."

Before I can get out of the car, Heero is at my door grabbing my backpack and walking me to the front door of the house. Putting my bag down he reaches out and hugs me, and I don't pull away. We stand in an embrace, not awkward at all, for at least two minutes. My heart, head, and emotions betray me. I feel something. And when he kisses my forehead, I almost melt right here at the door.

"See you tomorrow. And Nandi, debutantes are overrated." He turns and walks away. I fumbled with the keys praying he will just drive off. But he sits there, waiting for me to go in. I am so rattled. It takes me a few tries to finally open the door.

CHAPTER THREE

"Good morning. Thanks for picking me up for school. Last night was bananas. Pops got sick out of nowhere and had to be rushed to the hospital. It was super late when we finally made it home. I didn't want to disturb Daddy this morning, and there was no way I was going to get up on time to catch the bus."

"No problem. I'm glad you called. I have something for you and was trying to figure out how I could get it to you before the end of school." Heero handed me a kit a little smaller than a pencil pouch.

"Are you kidding me? A screwdriver, screws and pads and oil," I laughed. "You're too kind. How could I ever repay you?"

"If you're going to keep wearing that steel trap of

a brace, you at least need the proper tools, and you should do better at maintaining it. I know a guy I can call and have him tighten everything up for you. I mean if you want me to."

That was the sweetest thing anyone has done for me. Heero saw what I needed and took action. But I can't bring myself to verbalize it. Instead, I place my hand on top of his resting on the gear shift. And we ride the rest of the way to school laughing about the day before, with his thumb rubbing the side of my hand.

The butterflies in my stomach, heart palpitations, and rush of warmth starting at the top of my head I felt yesterday returned. There is no mistaking, it is because of his touch, his presence, his smile and the way he looks at me. I don't want to figure out what this really is, I want to let it ride to see where this thing goes. If it's meant to be, it'll be. As soon as that thought entered my brain, I hear that Florida Georgia line song playing in my head, and I kind of bop along with it in my seat. Is it just me, or does anyone else have a soundtrack to their lives that magically plays in times like these?

Heero parks in his usual spot in the student parking lot, grabs my backpack and we walk across the street to the campus. "See ya later sweet potato." Heero hands me my backpack and we part ways.

"You just missed the exit! Where are we going, Heero? I told you I'm tired and just want to go home! Coach pushed me extra hard today in workouts!" I yell, looking at the exit that leads to my house.

"Relax already. You don't have to always be in control of everything. I know you're tired and have put in hard work to get back to playing condition. So, I have a surprise I think you might like."

"Surprise, huh? This better not be any funny business. Mrs. Everette dumped a boat load of work on us today, and I have no time for games."

"No games, I promise. Give me about fifteen more minutes and we will arrive at our destination." Heero smiles watching for my reaction.

"Arrive at our destination? What are you up to?" I laughed. "We've passed The Trails, and Jackson Heights. That means we're going to The Valley, because I know you're not taking me to Harbor Springs. Neither one of us got any business in the Harbor Springs and those uppity folks don't want us out there any way. Last week a group of kids got locked up for riding around out there."

"For your information, we are going to the Harbor Springs."

"Heero, don't get me locked up. No basketball team will want me with an arrest record. And you know my dad will kill me and you." Although I am surprised, and nervous that we are actually going to Harbor Springs, I am also a little excited. Harbor Springs is a suburb of Caledonia, where the elite live and play. As a special treat, my dad and I used to drive out there and look at the huge houses, excuse me, the *estates*, and fantasize about living there.

"My dad has a client, Mr. William Harshaw who runs marathons. In fact, last year he ran in the New York and Boston Marathons. He heard I was training for the upcoming Caledonia Marathon and invited me to his home. He wants to talk about the marathon, my plans for after graduation and beyond. He said I could bring a friend, and that's you."

"Really? We're going to his house? Why didn't you give me a heads up or something?" I reach into my bag to find a lip gloss, brush, and anything else to help me look more presentable.

"Nandi, you're fine. Really. You are fine!"

I hate it when he does that. It's embarrassing and I

don't know what to do with his comments, so I ignore them. It's also obvious Heero likes me, but I really want the two of us to be just friends and not over complicate things. He's been there for me after my surgery, and especially since working out together. He said my books were too heavy to lug around on crutches and carried them between classes.

"After my injury, the only support system I had were my parents. All my friends kept going about their day to day as usual. No one helped me, or even asked if I needed help. When I couldn't hang out and do the normal teenaged things, I became withdrawn and depressed, suffering in silence. I didn't want that for you," Heero said when I asked him why he would be so nice.

He has been there for me in ways I didn't know I needed. And I'm thankful. I try to act like I don't hear his little remarks, like *you're fine*; *if I were your man*; and my personal favorite, *if you'd let me love you*. Heero is really sweet, but I don't want to blur the lines of our friendship. He's used to getting what he wants, his family is rich and super connected. His dad is a partner in his family's law firm. It's one of the largest in Caledonia and his mother is a judge. Although they don't live in Harbor Springs, their neighborhood in Jackson Heights is not shabby at all.

The few times I've visited his home, his dad was super nice. But his mom on the other hand was nice nasty. She smiled and hugged me, but I felt like she was also judging me. From the little things she says, lets me know she thinks I don't measure up to their standards. I'm not a debutante, and my dad is not a part of certain circles. Which is not a problem. Friends we are, and friends we will be.

"You have got to be kidding me! This house. Heero, this has to be the most beautiful house I've ever seen, and we haven't seen the inside yet. I cannot believe we are about to go into this house. It's breath taking." I am in awe of the most amazing house I have ever seen. The long driveway adds to the drama and allure. I am mesmerized to say the least.

"Welcome, to our home," Mr. Harshaw smiles opening the huge iron doors and greeting us with the warmest smile. "Did you find us okay?"

"Thank you for having us, you gave perfect directions. This is my friend, Nandi Cooper. Nandi, Mr. William Harshaw," Heero, the perfect gentleman, introduces us. I'm taken by Mr. Harshaw, a tall thin and lanky man. His arms are long, with huge hands at the end of them. I wouldn't have taken him for a marathon runner. An athlete for sure, but basketball over running.

"Please come in," Mr. Harshaw invites us into the foyer. I feel like I've stepped into a magazine. Looking around with my mouth open, I'm taking in the detail of the craftsmanship and décor. With Heero's hand in the small of my back, I don't know if he is guiding me or holding me up. We follow Mr. Harshaw through his gigantic home and stop in a room with floor to ceiling windows, beautiful plants and a small feast. "Help yourself, I took the liberty of putting together snacks. And don't be shy."

Snacks he said. This spread is more than *snacks*. There is so much he must be expecting more company. I don't want to seem greedy, but I'm always hungry after a workout. With my eyes as big as my stomach, I'm reminded of a story Gigi tells often. Her family was invited to a cookout. She piled her plate up with all the delicious looking food she thought she wanted and realized looks can be deceiving. Gigi's mom made her eat everything on her plate. So, I'll just put a few things on mine.

"Thank you very much for the hospitality," I thank our host, and give Heero the eye.

"Oh yeah, thanks," Heero nudges me.

"You're most welcome, eat as much as you want," Mr. Harshaw sat at the table watching us contemplate our choices. "How's the training going, Heero? Are you ready for your very first full marathon? My nerves almost got the better of me my first time. The night before I went back and forth with myself about not competing at all. What was I thinking? And who do I think I am, I thought. But my wife reminded me how hard I worked and who I am. I laced up my shoes and hit the pavement. The nerves melted away, and it was nonstop from there."

"Training is going good, and honestly, I'm very nervous about running a full marathon for the first time. It's double the distance of the half," Heero laughed nervously. "Why aren't you running this year?"

Although Heero is making a joke, I can hear the jitters in his voice.

"I've been so busy with a couple of projects that I haven't had time to train. An old man like myself needs all the training I can get before trying to run," Mr. Harshaw laughed. Enough about us, Nandi, what a beautiful name for a beautiful young lady. Of course, I already know this guy. His dad and I go back a long way. Right now, I'm more interested in what you see in his fat head," Mr. Harshaw jokes. "Seriously tell me about yourself. What are your plans for after graduation, your interests?"

"Hmm," I thought for a second. Mr. Harshaw

caught me off guard, I'm just a third wheel here today, and was not expecting to be interviewed. "There's not much to tell, not much at all. First, Heero and I are friends. He's been a great support since my ACL surgery, always pushing me to dig deeper, and go a little further for maximum progress. Secondly, my plans are to attend a division one university and play basketball, take on a double major in English and Communications, and afterwards attend law school and become a sports agent."

Heero is smiling and taking it all in, as if he is seeing me for the first time. His looks, like his comments, I ignored but take note.

"Division one basketball, a double major, law school and sports management. I am impressed." Clapping and head cocked to the side, Mr. Harshaw gives me a look more of shock than being impressed. "It's not often that I meet young people who know exactly what they want. Very ambitious, obviously smart, and pretty. Are you planning to run the marathon with Heero?"

"Ambition: a strong desire to do or achieve something, requiring determination and hard work. My father has drilled it into me," I ramble off the definition. "Heero and I have been training together, but I'm planning to participate in the 5K. It's part of my rehab to get back to basketball one-hundred-percent."

"Basketball, huh? No way. Let me see what you've got," Mr. Harshaw said, getting up from the table. "I know a little something about basketball. I used to play in high school and college."

"What do you mean, show you what I've got?"

"Just like I said. Follow me."

Heero nods at me, and we get up from the table and follow Mr. Harshaw out the huge sliding glass doors onto a patio and around to the backyard to find the most beautiful basketball court I've seen. "Heads up!" he yells. And I catch the ball he hurls my way.

"Show me what you've got Miss Cooper," he says again, taking his defense stance, with one hand in my face.

"Take him, Nandi," Heero urges.

Hesitating, unsure of myself, I take a deep breath and drive in. Mr. Harshaw lunges for the ball. I dribble and spin past him, going in for the layup. Nervous sweat rolls down my back. Retrieving the ball, I throw it to Mr. Harshaw and get on the ready to play defense.

He dribbles, and fakes like he's going left. Keeping my eyes on the ball I wait and make my move. I drive in and steal the ball, making a fast break to the goal. Executing one of my well-rehearsed moves, I pull up. Step back. Shoot and score.

"Nice! Real nice!" Mr. Harshaw shouts. "You're a pretty good baller."

Out of nowhere, Heero runs to me picks me up and swings me around. I'm confused and looking at him to understand what's really going on. He's smiling at me like someone crazy.

"What? What's wrong with you?" I ask still in the air.

"You're not wearing your brace," Heero laughs. "You took him, making cuts and moves. I knew you didn't need that contraption. It's been holding you back."

Without thinking about it, I plant a kiss on Heero. Then another and another. Short quick kisses. And this time it was him that didn't pull away. In fact, Heero kisses me back, welcoming my kisses.

"She's everything you said, Heero," Mr. Harshaw says walking over to us.

"What do you mean, everything he said?" I ask quickly looking from Heero to Mr. Harshaw, waiting for an answer from either one of them.

"I ran into Mr. Harshaw at my dad's office, we were talking about the marathon and training. He also mentioned his Alma Mater, Dowdy State University, and his ties to their athletic program. When he invited me over, I had an idea. I told him about you, how good you are in basketball, your injury and your situation. I asked if he could help by talking to the coaches on your behalf."

I'm standing here embarrassed and feeling ambushed, and it's showing on my face.

"It was as innocent as he said, I'm sorry if you feel deceived. But I do think you have something to offer the women's basketball team. Tell you what I can do. I'll give the head coach a call and get the two of you connected. I'll also call the directors of recruitment, development and alumni affairs to see what scholarships are available. Heero says you're super smart, we should be able to help you get most, if not all, of your school paid for."

"Thank you. Thank you so much, Mr. Harshaw. You'd do that for me, without knowing me?" I ask, confused.

"You're a friend of Heero's, and I am a friend of his dad's, which makes him a friend of mine. We take care of each other. So, yes. I'd do that for you. Consider it done."

Sticking my hand out to shake his, Mr. Harshaw takes my hand and pulls me into him. "I'm a hugger. And you're more than welcome."

Mr. Harshaw releases, and Heero grabs me. This time his hug is to make sure we are okay. I want to be upset, but I can see his intentions were not to hurt or embarrass me, but to help. I give him a squeeze of confirmation. "Thanks, Heero," I whisper.

CHAPTER FOUR

"I see you're not wearing it today. Did you leave your brace at home?" Heero asks, pulling out of the student parking lot on our way to train.

"I have it in my backpack, just in case. Seriously, did you think I was going to leave home without it? It's my insurance," I said looking in the back seat where we threw our things when getting in the car.

"Of course, you have it with you." He laughs and reaches for my hand. I quickly start fumbling in my purse, looking for absolutely nothing, in an effort to keep my hands busy. "I was really proud of you yesterday. You've come a long way in your recovery, and playing Mr. Harshaw like you did, without your brace was a major breakthrough."

"Yeah, thank you for introducing me to Mr.

Harshaw. He's a really nice guy, and if he can do what he said, I'll be set for college. I can't tell you how big of a burden will be lifted."

"In talking to him, one thing led to another. He mentioned his Alma Mater and it made perfect sense to bring you into the conversation. You know I've got your back, right?" Heero interrupted.

"Since my surgery and all, you've really been there for me. I'm grateful for everything. Honestly, I don't know what me and my dad would have done without you." Sifting in my seat I'm trying to find a way to change the subject. Looks like I just have to rip the bandage off and get it out there, and over with. "Heero, I want to apologize for kissing you the way I did. I got overly excited when you pointed out me playing without my brace. I know how important the marathon is to you and staying focused on your training. It's not my intention to disrupt that or be a distraction. Besides, we both have so much going on. To be honest, I got caught up in the moment. And the kiss didn't mean anything. Right?"

"Yeah. Okay. Right," Heero responds never taking his eyes off the road.

"That's it?" I don't know what I was expecting Heero to say, but *yeah, okay, right* was not it. *Did I want him to make a case? Or at least say the kiss meant something to him?*

"Yep. That's it."

We ride in silence. I want to look over at him but wouldn't dare. Making it to our running spot Heero gets out and throws me the keys.

"Wait. Aren't you going to stretch, and wait for me?" I yell before he shuts the door.

"You've got this. Besides, I warmed up while I waited for you after school," he said just before closing the door harder than usual, but not slamming it.

Sitting here, I'm almost shocked. Heero runs off, and I get out of the car and put my ear buds in. After stretching, I start walking my route. Heero, has never left me behind like he did today. We usually stretch together, and he walks with me for five minutes before he runs a head. Today, is a six-mile run for him, and a two mile walk for me.

I have to shake off the stuff I'm feeling about Heero's reaction, or lack thereof. After all, we're just friends. *Inhale, exhale. Inhale, exhale.* Listening to the sound of the music, I breathe, getting into my zone. Before I know it, I'm back at the car and waiting for Heero.

It usually takes me about thirty minutes to walk

two miles, and Heero forty minutes to run six miles. But today, I'm waiting longer, much longer for him to return. Concerned, I get out of the car and look in the direction he should be coming. With no sign of him, I get nervous and a knot forms in the pit of my stomach. My gut tells me to walk in the direction he should be coming to look for him. But if he shows up from another direction and I'm not here he might be concerned. So, I sit on the hood, and keep watch like a meerkat.

Finally, I see him round the corner a half mile away, I breathe deep. Letting out a sigh of relief, I stand up, and wait impatiently for him to reach the car.

Heero stretches, and doesn't say a word, or acknowledge that I'm standing here looking at him with my hands on my hips. Realizing it's up to me to say something I jump right in. "What took you so long? I was worried sick."

"My apologies. There is so much going on in my head, and I got caught up in the moment. The run was so exciting and before I knew it, I'd run a few extra miles." Tinkering with his app on his watch, Heero used my words on me.

"Yeah. Okay. Right." I look at him sideways, get

in the car and gently close the door and wait for him to finish stretching.

We ride in silence all the way to my house. Before he could barely come to a stop, I reach between the seats, grabbing my backpack and get out of the car.

"Nandi," Heero calls to me. "I won't be able to work out tomorrow. I'll be busy."

CHAPTER FIVE

"Hi Nandi, this is William, William Harshaw. I hope you don't mind me calling, Heero gave me your number. I just want you to know I spoke with Coach Terrell, and he's very interested in talking to you about playing at DSU. He will be giving you a call this evening. And be on the lookout for scholarship information."

"Thank you, for all your help, Mr. Harshaw. I cannot thank you enough."

"I told you before, you are a friend of Heero, that means I consider you a friend. And we take care of each other."

"I'll remember that. Mr. Harshaw can I ask you a question?"

"Of course."

"When did you talk to Heero?"

"Just a few minutes ago, actually."

"Okay, great."

I haven't talked to or seen Heero for two weeks, but I didn't want Mr. Harshaw to know, and obviously Heero didn't mention it either. The day he dropped me off at my house and said he wouldn't be able to work out the next day was the last I've seen or heard from him. We haven't run into each other at school either. Although we don't have any classes together, and don't normally see each other at school, I've been looking for him.

Mr. Harshaw came through just like he said he would. And thirty minutes after speaking to him Coach Terrell called from Dowdy State University.

"Hi Nandi, this is Coach Terrell, you can call me Coach T. I had a conversation with a good friend, William Harshaw and we've recently acquired film of you playing from your high school coach, Coach Pratt. I have to say, I'm impressed with your athletic ability, academics as well as the great things Coach Pratt and your teachers have to say about you. We are in need of a shooting guard with your skill set, and I would like to offer you a scholarship to play at Dowdy State University. I also understand you've been fighting to come back from an ACL injury, and are almost in playing condition. What do you think about joining our team?"

"Oh wow! I don't know what to say." I was holding back tears.

"How about this. You come for an official visit soon, see how you like things, and make your decision afterwards."

"That sounds like a plan. Thank you so much for considering me, and even wanting to take a chance on me, Coach T."

"Thank Mr. Harshaw, I did. He's responsible for making this match."

Actually, it's Heero that's responsible. Excited, I find my phone to call him. I want to share with him my news.

"Hello," Heero's deep, but not too deep voice answered on the first ring.

"Hey. I've got great."

"Sorry, you've reached the voice mail of Heero Ibeh. Leave a message and I'll get back with you soon."

Crap. I want Heero to be the first to know about my offer, and he didn't answer. It's been a little over an hour since I talked with Mr. Harshaw, and he had just talked to Heero. I feel like he's avoiding me. Before a couple of weeks ago, Heero was always available for me. Truth be told, I miss talking to him, working out together, and I even miss his annoying laugh. Most of all, I miss my friend, and his caring nature. And I've never admitted it. My dad will have to do.

"Hey big guy, I've got great news," I joined Daddy on the couch.

"I can use some of that right about now." Daddy paused his movie.

"I just got a call, and a scholarship offer from the Dowdy State University women's basketball team. Coach T wants me to come for an official visit. And I'll be getting more information about scholarships as well."

"That's the best news I've heard in a very long time, Sugar. Congratulations." Daddy leans over to kiss my head. "How did this come about? Dowdy State is not one I've heard you talk about before."

"Remember I told you about the guy Heero introduced me to? He made a few calls, and the rest is history as they say." I dance around waving my hands in the air.

"Heero? That's my guy. Tell him I said thanks, and good looking out."

"I would, but I haven't seen him in two weeks,

and when I tried to call, it went straight to voice mail." I sat back down confiding in Daddy.

"Wow," Daddy makes a painful face. "What did you do Nandi?"

"It's like that? You're just gonna assume I did something? You're my dad, you're supposed to side with me."

"Yes, I'm your dad, and I know you." Daddy tapped my nose. "So, are you going to tell me what happened?"

"I kinda got excited about playing Mr. Harshaw in a one-on-one game. I know I've played the game thousands of times. But I did without my brace, and Daddy you should have seen me. I didn't hold back. Frankly, I forgot I didn't have my brace on. When Heero got all excited about me playing without it, I got excited too," I take a deep breath, "and I kissed him."

"You did what? I thought *you* said you two are just friends?" Daddy looks confused.

"But that's not all. The next day I apologized and told him I got overly excited, didn't want to be a distraction, or be distracted. And that the kiss didn't mean anything." I cringed hearing the words coming out of my mouth.

"Ouch, Nandi. Why didn't you just shoot him and

put him out of his misery?" Daddy laughed. "Let me tell you something. Heero maybe *just* a friend to you. Any man, young or old, that has gone above and beyond for you the way he has, has more than *just friends* feelings for you. He is making an investment in you, with one day banking on a payoff. I would say the payoff he's looking for is a real relationship. Do you understand what I'm saying? Sugar, I know you have issues with people getting too close, and it comes from your mother leaving and not being around. Heero's not your Mom, and sooner or later if you don't trust someone with your heart, you're going to be bitter."

"I hear what you're saying. But I just want to be friends, and right now I miss my friend."

"Call him, Nandi. It's as simple as picking up the phone."

"I tried to call to tell him my good news, but he wouldn't answer. It went straight to voicemail. And you're right, I owe Heero a real apology. But how when I can't reach him to tell him either?"

"You'll figure it out. Now hand me the remote so I can finish this movie."

Walking away from Dad, I thought about what he said about my Mom. When I was ten years old, she decided she didn't want to be a mom or wife anymore. Just picked up and walked off, leaving my dad to pick up the pieces. For a very long time I thought I was the reason she left, but as I've gotten older and watched a lot of *Iyanla, Fix My Life*, I realize she's the broken one. Not me. But it's been hard not to feel cracked at least when all my friends have a mom, and I don't.

CHAPTER SIX

It's signing day at Caledonia High School, and the entire school is buzzing. We have seventeen athletes signing from various sports including basketball, track and field, softball, baseball, football and volleyball. They're signing with four-year colleges and universities from division one through junior colleges. Every athlete signing is sitting at beautifully decorated table, with coaches, family, and friends. Dad and Gigi are here, and Pops sends his love from home. My high school coach, Coach Pratt, and teammates, and Coach T drove in from Dowdy State University to be here for my signing.

When my dad and I went to DSU I fell in love with the campus, the atmosphere, and the academics they have to offer. The team made me feel welcome, and the school felt like I belonged. It was everything Mr. Harshaw said it would be. He even arranged for me and my dad to enjoy the city while we were there. We had a great time, and I look forward to spending the next four years there.

The gym is filled with students, family, friends, and media for Caledonia High School's signing day. Each year a big deal is made of the event, and this one is every bit as amazing as the past. As happy as I am about the signing, I'm sad that I still haven't talked to Heero. It's evident that he's blocked my call and he's avoiding me. The smile on my face is not as genuine as it can be.

"Who do you keep looking around the gym for?" Gigi whispered in my ear.

"No one," I lied. "There are just so many people in the stands. I'm just taking it all in."

"I'm sure he's here." My Dad hugged me tight. "I'm proud of you, my favorite daughter."

"Dad, I'm your only daughter." I laugh. He always knows how to lighten the mood and make me feel better. Looking at all the support I have sitting with me and standing behind me I have to smile. And just in time, the newspaper's photographer snaps a picture. I pray he didn't catch me with an awkward look on my face. I am the world's worst when it comes to taking pictures. There are albums full of pictures to prove it.

"He could have warned us that he was about to take the picture. I didn't get a chance to flash my good smile," Gigi fusses, and everyone at the table laughs. Every picture she takes she has the exact same smile. It's by design, and she's worked hard at perfecting it. Maybe I should take lessons from her.

"Thanks for letting me be a part of your big day, Nandi, and I look forward to catching you play at DSU wearing the burgundy and gold." Mr. Harshaw hugs me and shakes my dad's hand. "Terrell, take good care of this one, she's something special."

I watch Mr. Harshaw walk across the crowded gym floor and walking toward him from the opposite direction is Heero. They shake hands and embrace. Over Mr. Harshaw's shoulder Heero looks up and we make eye contact.

"Where are you going?" Gigi asks as I walk away from my table, making my way through the crowd.

"I'll be right back," I tell her and motion with my hand.

Instead of going in a straight line to where the two of them stood moments earlier, I make my way to the door near the concession stand, in an effort to catch

Heero dipping out to avoid me and going out the door on the opposite side of the gym floor.

"Hey there," I catch Heero's jacket, stopping him in his tracks.

"Hey," Heero shoved his hands deep into his pockets, looking everywhere but at me.

"Can we talk?" I ask.

"I have to go. I'm —."

"Just for a few minutes, I'll be brief, I promise. Let's step outside." I hold the door open for him and he walks through, then posts up on the brick wall just outside of the door with his back and right foot on the wall. "I haven't seen you around, and I just want to say thank you. Without you, none of this would be possible."

I reach out and hug Heero. When he wrapped his arms around me, I had that feeling again. It's almost electric.

"You're welcome, it's nothing," he said pulling away.

"How's the ACT prep going? Are you still planning to take the test this weekend?"

"The prep is going so-so. Yeah, I'm taking the test."

"Remember to dress for business and eat a banana before going. They're supposed to help with memory or something. I read it somewhere, and don't really know if it works or not. But it's worth a shot. And how's the training going?"

"I guess you've stopped training?" Heero answers my question with a question.

"And why would you guess that? I haven't missed a day of training. In fact, I'm still following the plan you gave me. I'm seeing this race through. I've come too far to not finish. Heero, I've really missed my friend," I explain.

Stepping away from the wall, Heero looks me in the eyes, "If you haven't guessed, I like you Nandi. And when you apologized for kissing me, I was crushed. Because I felt stupid for thinking you were finally feeling me the way I feel you.

"I've always wanted to be more than your friend. When I ran those extra miles the last time, I saw you, I made up in my mind that I could no longer be your friend, if I can't have more. I've done everything to avoid seeing you, even in my dreams. I changed where I park, where I run, and I've even changed that goofy ring tone you set on my phone. Unsuccessfully, I've tried to erase you from my memory, but nothing has worked. Knowing how important today is for you, I couldn't miss it, but I didn't want you to see me, or come face to face with you.

"Standing here with you right now, I've realized something else. Since what we have is the start of nothing, I'm okay with being your friend. If that's the only way to have you in my life, I'm willing to just be your friend."

"Heero, I've been looking all over for you. Come on, we're going to be late," a familiar voice said behind me.

It was Sunni. She has been stalking Heero since tenth grade. She's sent him notes, made him cookies and when he was playing football, she even had a shirt made with his number on it. He used to make all the excuses to keep from talking to her, going out with her, and even being her friend. Now, they're a thing? No way.

"I'll talk to you later," Heero said walking off with her.

I'm standing here with my mouth open, watching them walk away. Wondering what just happened, I'm feeling lower than I ever have.

"Ain't that some bull," Emily said walking up to me. "You let him go, and now he's with Sunni. Of all the people to lose your man to. Go ahead, pick your face up. I'll wait."

"Will you shut up!" I turn to look at Emily. "First

of all. Heero is not my boyfriend, for the millionth time. And secondly, Sunni? Like for real, Sunni."

"Gigi sent me to find you. And if I come back without you, she's going to have both of our heads. Pick your face up and figure out how you're going to get your man back."

"Didn't I tell you to shut up! Dang Emily, you really talk too much."

"Okay. Okay. But I have one more thing to say."

"What Emily?"

"Sunni gotcho man!" Emily cracks up at herself.

CHAPTER SEVEN

"Attention! Attention, everyone! May I have your attention please!" Enzo, our senior class president yelled into the bull horn. "Thank you, and welcome to the class of 2021's senior fun night. Give it up to our sponsors for making this event possible, and the Caledonia Heights Mall for hosting our Senior Scavenger Hunt. We have the mall to ourselves this evening. While our vice president, Brees, is making her way to the microphone to give us ground rules and announcements, D.J. drop the beat!"

The mob of seniors go wild. A few of our classmates jump on stage and hype the crowd further. We're all swagging and surfing, dancing and singing along following their promptings.

"Thank you, D.J." Brees motions for the D.J. to cut the music. "Like Enzo said, I have a few announcements and ground rules:

1. You will have thirty minutes to complete the scavenger hunt.
2. Each team should have a receipt with the items you must find. Teams must stay together, there is no divide and conquer for this challenge.
3. You must take a picture if you don't have the physical item.
4. No breaking any laws.
5. No cheating.
6. And last but not least, let's have fun.

After the scavenger hunt is over, food and drinks will be served, along with dancing at the food court."

"You heard the lady! Now, let's have a good time!" Enzo shouts into the microphone over Brees's shoulder, and we scramble like ants whose mound was just kicked in.

My teammates and I have been looking forward to the senior class fun night all week. It was a no brainer, the four of us were going to make up our scavenger hunt team. We're all very competitive, and we came to win.

"First things first. What's on our list?" Emily asks. She's the captain of the basketball team and is a natural leader. "We need to know what we're working with and make a plan of what stores to hit."

"Great idea," Pixie agrees. She goes along with everything Emily says.

Amber has the list and starts reading. "Our list is a combination of pictures and items to find.

1. A picture of one of us wearing something patriotic.
2. We need a makeup sample.
3. A picture of one of us wearing a baseball cap and waving a team pennant.
4. A baby rattle.
5. Find a salesperson wearing a blue shirt."

"Okay, let's get started," Emily barks.

"What about the rest of the list?" I ask.

"You keep up with the list. Once we find these five things, you should have an idea for the next five. Amber you take the pictures. Now bring it in. Hustle on three," Emily responds as if she's running point on the basketball court. And we fall right in.

Our first find is a makeup sample. Next, Emily dresses in a red, white, and blue star-spangled t-shirt we found in *All American Apparel*. Amber can barely take the picture for laughing at Emily's medium size body in an extra small t-shirt. The baseball cap and pennant, along with the salesperson wearing a blue shirt… Easy-peasy. But the baby rattle not so much. We're running from the third floor to the first. Pixie was certain a few minutes ago she knew exactly where we can find one. No such luck.

"We'll come back to the baby rattle. How are we doing on time? And what's next on the list?" Emily asks.

"We have twenty minutes." Pixie, our official timekeeper looks at her watch.

"Next on our list is a group selfie with an item that begins with 'J' and Heero?"

"Heero, Nandi. Seriously." Amber laughs.

"No, what I meant to say is, we need to find a blinged out belt buckle," I straighten up my response, and turn to watch Heero scramble with his team down the escalator, while we're running up the stairs out of his line of sight.

Heero is with his friends, and Sunni is not with him.

"I know exactly where we can find it!" Pixie snaps. "My aunt bought one just a few weeks ago to go with an outfit she was putting together. And please don't ask."

We laugh and follow Pixie to a little store, tucked in a short hallway near the bathrooms at the end of the mall I never knew existed.

"Five minutes," Pixie announces. "We have five minutes."

Taking the picture in a hurry, we turn and sprint to the check point, to be counted for the competition. And we make it just in time, without ever finding the baby rattle.

"I'm going to grab us a table," I leave the team, waiting for the judges to check and certify our finds. I chose a table out of the way so I can people watch. Honestly, to watch for one person in particular, Heero.

"I saw you sprinting down the hall, like a track star," Heero sneaks up behind me, and takes a seat at the table. "Your leg is doing pretty good, I see."

"Yes, very good in fact. Yoshi said I finished therapy much better than expected. Thanks to the extra work I was doing with a friend. It's doing so good in fact, instead of walking the 5K, I plan to run the 10K."

"What? Way to go Nandi! I am really proud of you."

"So, where's your girlfriend? I mean your teammates?" I asked, sorry not sorry for the accidental on purpose slip of the tongue.

"My team is at the table with the judges. I saw you over here by yourself, and thought I'd come say hi. Girl friend? I have no idea who you're talking about. I'm here with my boys."

"Your girlfriend, Sunni," I press the issue.

"Sunni? What in the? What would possess you think Sunni of all girls, would be my girlfriend? And you know she's stalked me since tenth grade. Ohhh," Heero started laughing. "Signing day. You have got to be kidding me. Surely, you didn't think me and Sunni. Wow, Nandi you cut me deep, thinking I'd stoop that low. Actually, we were headed to the final ACT prep class, and she asked if she could get a ride. Actually, Principal Wilks asked if I could give her a ride."

I want to slide right out of my chair, onto the floor, and out the door. But I laugh right along with Heero. He changes the subject, and we talk like it had not been more than a month since we chatted like this.

"Are you ready for the race next weekend?" I ask.

"Yes. Well, I will be. I tweaked my hamstring, a couple weeks ago, and I've been treating it and doing a modified training schedule. Would you like to train together this last week?" he asks. "We can run in our regular place."

"I'd like that." I smile.

"What are you two doing way over here hiding in the back of the food court?" Emily asks. The rest of our team, and Heero's friends with her.

"How'd we do? Did we win?" I ask.

"The Geek Squad beat us by two," Pixie laughs, sliding a small envelope across the table to me. "But we did get gift cards. Each one of us for a different store in the mall. I'm not even mad, this is the most fun I've had in a long time. I've worked up an appetite, and they're setting up a nice taco bar."

"We'll get out of your way, and grab our own table," Heero said standing up.

"For what? Grab a couple of those tables and add them to ours, the more the merrier. Right ladies," Amber winks at me.

Heero's friends pull up two more tables, and chairs and we laugh, talk, and eat, enjoying each other's company.

"Alright class of 2021!" Enzo yells from the bull horn. "It's time to get your party on, D.J. turn it up!"

Everyone leaves their seats, and the food court turns into a dance floor.

"Would you like to dance?" Heero asks extending his hand.

"Maybe one. Then I really need to head home. I gotta get my rest, I'm running a race next weekend." I smile and take his hand.

As soon as we get to the dance floor, the D.J. switches things up and plays Kavery's slow and super sexy *Stay The Night*. Heero pulls me in close to him and wraps his arms around me. I feel his warmth, smell the citrus notes of his cologne, and feel his heart keeping beat with the snaps in the sultry and highly hypnotic music. My heart, my head, and my emotions are betraying me yet again. That something I'm feeling in the pit of my stomach is not the tacos. And I don't know what to do with these feelings except continue to press them down into the deepest parts of me. The last time my feelings surfaced, I apologized for them and hurt my friend. Until I know for sure what I'm feeling for Heero, it's best I play it cool.

"What's the matter? You okay?" Heero asks, stepping back.

"It's been a long day, and I should probably go home."

"Your girls don't look like they're ready to head

out. If you don't mind, I can take you home. I should probably get some rest myself."

"Are you sure? I don't want you to go out of your way."

"Seriously. It's not a problem. Besides, it'll give us time to catch up."

"Now, you want to catch up with a sister," I bump him, and smile. "Just let me tell my girls I'm leaving with you."

Heero and I maneuver through the crowd to find Emily, Pixie, and Amber circled around Enzo, dancing and having the time of their lives. Standing there watching them I realize this will all come to an end real soon. We will all go our separate ways. Emily and I are going to four-year universities to play basketball, Pixie is off to Army bootcamp. And Amber is moving to Los Angeles to start an acting career. She's done commercials and plays since she was a kid. Her mom thinks she should make the move right after high school instead of waiting.

"Did we not say we come together and leave together before we got out of the car? And here you are ditching us. Nandi, this is our time," commander in chief Emily fusses.

"Give it a rest, Em. Nandi you go ahead, we're

good." Pixie came to my rescue. "And don't go straight home."

Rolling my eyes and sticking out my tongue Heero and I walk away from my friends and past the D.J.'s booth to the exit.

"Do you need to make any stops before heading home?" Heero asks like the perfect gentleman he is.

"Since you asked, I'd love a scoop of rainbow sherbet on a sugar cone."

"Do you realize what time it is? It's after eleven, and no ice cream shops open," Heero laughs and shakes his head at my request.

"That new truck stop on the highway is open. They have the best rainbow sherbet. And it's on the way," I smile and give him the puppy dog eyes, and pouty lips.

"Ice cream it is," Heero starts the car.

Truthfully, I'm extremely tired, but I don't want the night to end. Ice cream is the perfect excuse to spend more time with Heero, away from our friends and classmates, noise, and chaos. And I don't think he minds the time we're spending sitting in the very last booth out of the way, with our legs wrapped under the table, laughing and talking as our ice cream melts.

"Is everything okay? What's this all about?" I ask Heero, after he gets me out of class with a pass from Coach Pratt.

"Just follow me," Heero starts walking.

"Coach Pratt's office is the other way," I stop.

"Will you just follow me already? And stop being difficult." He laughs and shakes his head.

I follow Heero into the back stairs near my classroom. Looking around to see if anyone else is in the stairway, he stops and sits down on the landing between floors. I take my cue and sit next to him. Not saying a word, I watch and wait to find out what we're doing here.

"You've probably figured out by now, that Coach Pratt didn't send for you. I asked if I could go to the counselor's office and he was more than willing to give me a pass," Heero starts explaining. "Nandi, you've worked so hard to rehab your knee, and only started training for the 5K as a part of that process. Not only will you run on Saturday, but you've exceeded your expectations and going to run a 10K instead. I'm extremely proud of the effort, sacrifice, and time you've put into training even though running is not your sport of choice. Not many people would push themselves so hard to do something different and succeed the way you have. The race is in five days, and I have something I want to give you. I was going to wait till after school before our workout, but I can't wait."

Heero hands me a little box, and I'm not sure what to make of it. Several things go through my mind, as I try and figure out what could be in this rectangular box. Shaking it next to my ear, I listen for clues. And peer at it again, as if I have X-ray vision and can see through the white cardboard.

"Don't just sit there and look at the box, open it already," Hero urges.

"Umm, thank you," I said looking at the contents of the box and trying to sound grateful. "What are they exactly?"

"Shoe tags, dummy." You wear them like this, he

laughs lifting up his foot to show me his shoes. "A lot of runners wear them with motivational sayings, or 13.1 for the half marathon and 26.2 for the full. Go ahead, read the inscription."

"Fierce and strong," I say out loud. "Thank you so much, I love them. Do you really think I'm fierce and strong? And what's this symbol?" Heero had those words engraved on the metal tags, along with a symbol I've never seen before.

"Yes, and some. There are a lot of words I can use to describe how awesome you are, but I chose those two. They're what come to mind first. I've always thought highly of you, but during our time training together, I've gotten to know you better and what drives you. When you put your mind to it, there is no stopping you. I admire that in you, and I'm drawn to it as well.

"The symbol is called pempamsie, it's a symbol of strength from Ghana," Heero explains. "It also serves as a reminder that you have the strength within you to accomplish anything."

"That's so sweet, Heero. Again, thank you so much," I said, laying my head on his shoulder, and leaning into a hug as he puts his arm around me. We sit in silence, enjoying each other's company. Although no words are being spoken, plenty of communication is happening. It feels good to sit and feel his presence.

"You'd better get back to class, and I should probably stop by the counselors office before heading back to my class."

Heero stands and then helps me up. He's on the next step down, in front of me, bringing us face to face. Leaning into him lightly, I press my cheek into his. The electricity between us is undeniable. He wraps his arms around me, and I close my eyes, inhaling the essence of him, and snuggling closer into his neck. For a few seconds, I'm having an out-of-body experience. until footsteps at the bottom of the stairs, snaps me out of my trance.

"I'll see you after school," I said, before running back up the stairs. At the stairwell's entrance I turn around to see Heero still standing in the same spot watching me, and Basil Baits, who those footsteps belong to.

"If he don't know what to do with you in these stairs, I sure do," Basil smirks.

"Man, if you don't go on with that," Heero starts walking up one step at a time with his fists balled up.

"Chill man. I'm just kidding. I didn't know it was like that. Carry on."

And the bell rings. "Yeah, I'll see you after

school," Heero runs down the stairs the opposite way. We were in the stairwell for the last twenty minutes of class.

***

"I see you," Heero smiles from ear to year looking at my feet. "You didn't waist anytime putting the tags on your shoes. I was hoping to do that for you before we start our workout."

"Thanks again," I prance around kicking my feet up, showing off my tags like a little kid. "I really do like them. You put a lot of thought into this gift, and it means a lot. If you'd like, I can take them off so you can put them back on."

"You've got jokes, and you're welcome." Heero smiles, and shrugs like a little kid. "Will your family be at the race with you?"

"My dad, and Gigi will be there. Pops said he'll be cheering me on from home. Since being sick, he doesn't get out anymore. Gigi either records things for him, or FaceTimes him, so he feels like he's there. Because my mom is not around, sometimes my Dad can be a little overly supportive. He tries to be there enough for two parents. I'm not a little kid anymore missing my mommy, and I understand he can't do it all. With him helping Gigi take care of Pops, their expenses and trying to be everything for me, it's a bit much."

"You should be thankful that your dad not only wants to, but makes you a priority, even though he's a single dad, with a lot on his plate. I would give my right arm for my parents to be as supportive as your dad. They're always so busy with one thing or the other, their jobs, charities, or other obligations. I seem to be the very last thing on their list."

"Have your parents, or any of your family ever been to any of your races?" I questioned, feeling pretty low about even sounding like I was complaining about my dad.

"My granddad just gives me money. That's his answer and solution for everything. The things he wants to be bothered with and the things he doesn't. My brothers work in the family law firm and are under both my granddad and dad's thumbs. Tayo, the younger of my brother's tries to support me as much as he can. He'll probably be there."

"I'm sorry to hear that."

"It is what it is. I'm almost used to it."

"I'll be there cheering you on with a sign and yelling to the top of my lungs, after I'm done with the 10K."

"Not a sign," Heero laughs.

"Yep, a sign and all the bells and whistles. Oooo and a confetti popper when you cross the finish line. I'll go all out, like my mom used to. A super show of support." I parade around acting as if I'm carrying a sign, cheering, and mimicking exploding confetti with my hands.

"You wouldn't," Heero laughs at my animated show of support. The more he laughs the more I turn up the funny.

"I will and I am. That's what friends are for. You're going to get a real live Cooper celebration. My family is big on celebrating the little stuff, and the big stuff in a major way. And this my friend is big."

In this moment, I realize just how fortunate I am to have a family who celebrates my accomplishments no matter how small. Not all families are the same, or value each other the way we do.

"Well thank you friend, I look forward to crossing the finish line to such a spectacular celebration," Heero mocks, and we laugh all over again. "Can I ask you something? You don't mention your mother much. Every once in a while, in passing comments. Where is she, and why isn't she around?"

"My mom left us when I was ten years old. She didn't pack a bag or say goodbye. Later I did receive a letter explaining how much she loves me, and that she was just not cut out to be a mom. She asked for my forgiveness and that was that."

"I'm sorry," Heero said, opening my door, and throwing my backpack in the back seat.

"Sorry for what?" I question, turning to look at him before getting in the car.

"For not having your mom."

"Like I said, my dad overcompensates, and we've made it work without her. I'm good. Are we going to train today or what?" I didn't like where this conversation was headed and talking about my mom is not going to change anything.

CHAPTER NINE

"Are you okay?" Heero said pulling me up from my seat to hug and comfort me. "I'm so sorry to hear about your Pops. How's he doing?"

This time, his embrace didn't give me all the feels it gave me the last couple of times. It felt more friendly. Like a woo-woo-woo. Maybe because I'm worried. "All they've told us is that Pop's had a stroke, and he will pull through. But they also said they're running tests and have to assess any damage the stroke may have caused. As soon as they know more, they will share. Until then we're just praying and waiting."

"My mom always says, no news is good news," Heero said in an attempt to cheer me up.

I should have known. Every time I get overly excited, something comes along to humble me and brings me back down. Why wouldn't this time be any different? The race is in two days, and I'm feeling really confident about it. Plans for Heero's finish line celebration is in full swing and this happens.

"I was able to get in touch with your mom. She sends her love and prayers." Gigi said rubbing my shoulders on her way to the corner of the room to make calls to other family members.

"Okay," I groaned.

"Why would your Gigi call your mom? Aren't these your dad's parents? Does that mean she's coming?" Heero is full of questions.

"Actually, they're my mom's parents. And *she sends her love and prayers*, is code for she ain't coming."

"Wait, I don't understand," Heero pushed the issue. "I thought you said your dad helps take care of your grandparents."

"Yes. I did say that. It's really not as complicated as it sounds. When my parents got married, Pops and Gigi said they had the son they've always wanted. They've always treated him like their own. My Dad lost his parents as a teenager and took to them like real parents as well. When my mom left us, she left us all. Daddy kept doing what he's always done for them. It hurts Pops and Gigi that she left the way she did and stays away. They only call her when there is an emergency. And even though it's an emergency, she doesn't come. Gigi got real sick a few years ago, and doctors thought she might not make it. Pops called her, and she *sent her love and prayers* then too."

"Nandi that just sounds really odd. Don't you think?" Heero whispers, turning to look at me.

"Yes, I do. A woman walking away from her entire family is odd."

"That's not what I mean."

"What are you getting at?"

"A woman just up and walks away from her family, without taking anything or saying goodbye. I don't know about you, but that sends off red flags in my mind. Did someone take her? Is she in some type of institution? There seems like there is more going on."

"Slow your roll, future lawyer. Lower your red flags and relax. There is no mystery to solve, and I'm not interested in knowing why she felt the need to leave, other than what she initially said. I'm good, okay?"

"I just thought if you want to find her, my dad knows people."

"It's okay. I'm not broke, and don't need fixing. Years ago, I came to terms with it, and believe me I am good. But I thank you for your concern." I wrap my arm in his and lay my head on his shoulder, while we wait to hear something else about Pops. Every time a doctor or nurse comes around the corner Gigi jumps. Waiting is the worst part.

"Don't you guys have a race in two days that you need to be out walking, running, or doing something for?" Daddy asks joining us in the family waiting room. "It's going to be a little while before we know anything, and you don't have to sit here when you could be doing something else."

"I don't know if I should even compete in the race still." I admit.

"Oh no ma'am," Gigi joins the conversation. "I will not hear of it. Pops is going to pull through. He would not want you moping around and miss this race on account of him. You've come so far and trained so hard. You two go on. Get on out of here. If we hear anything at all, I'll call."

Heero grabs my hand and leads me out of the waiting room and to the elevators. Waiting for the elevator, he's watching me, and I stare straight ahead and pretend I don't notice. As soon as the elevator doors close, Heero pulls me to him and holds me tight. "Pops will be okay," he whispers, and kisses my forehead.

My heart jumps. Being in Heero's embrace and feeling his warm kisses lead from my forehead to my face, and finally stopping at my lips blur the lines of our friendship. The lines are blurred, smeared, smudged, and nearly erased. I give in to it all.

"You okay?" Heero says coming up for air, but still holding me.

I can't vocalize words, or sounds, I just nod. And Heero reaches over to push the button for the first floor.

***

Tomorrow is the day before the race, making it a rest day. That means today is the very last day of training, and we both have a short walk/run. Instead of going to our regular spot, Heero thought we should go to the race route and get a feel for it.

We strap on our running shoes, stretch, and just before we start walking, I say out loud, "Strong and fierce."

"Strong and fierce," Heero repeats smiling ear to

ear just before running ahead of me. "See you in a few."

Before I know it, my two miles of running and walking turn into an additional two more. With all that's going on with Pops, my walking, thinking, and talking to God takes me further than I intend. The change of location also plays a part in the extended distance. I noticed things that I may not on race day surrounded by the other runners. Things like the new mural on Spring Street leading to the historical district, and the painted fire hydrants. Thinking back, I try to remember if those hydrants were painted the last time Gigi and I drove through on one of her Sunday drives getting out of the house. The more I see, the more I am intrigued. A lot has been done to improve the look of the old Bailey Quarters. Pops says, "Back in the day, the Bailey Quarters was where Black folks shopped and owned businesses, because they weren't welcomed downtown."

The historical district was once Downtown Caledonia. Both are being restored separately. Downtown is being revived by the historical society, which is code for whites; and the Bailey Quarters by a Black collective group to preserve the culture of Caledonia. A culture that is a part of my family's heritage. Surprisingly, being in this part of town gave me such a peace.

I imagine what this place looked like as my Pops would say, *back in his day*, as well as when Bernie Cooper started Caledonia.

After the civil war Bernie Cooper was given forty acres by his former master. And with that forty acres he founded the town of Caledonia, naming it after his mother who he was sold away from her family when he was a child. In doing so, Caledonia's descendants will always have a way to return to her, for generations to come. The word is Bernie lost this part of Caledonia in a poker game to some White men. Pops says that's a lie. White men were not allowing blacks to play in their poker games. The truth is they threatened to burn down the entire town, and everyone in it if he didn't sell. The historical district, and the bordering neighborhood now called The Bottoms where many poor Blacks still live, is what they allowed Blacks to keep.

"Hey, how did I beat you back? I was about to come looking for you." Heero jogged to meet me.

"During my run, I started looking around, and walked off the route checking out the Bailey Quarters. I like what they're doing down there restoring buildings and creating a new space. It's going to be amazing when they're done."

"I heard there will be a statue of the founder Bernie Cooper in the square. You have the same last name. Is there any relation?"

"Actually, yes. It's my dad's family, but my pop's is somewhat of a history buff and has told me a lot about Caledonia's founder and what Blacks have had to deal with since its founding."

"That's really cool. Mr. Harshaw's architectural firm *Harshaw & Mosley* is heading up the renovations. I'm sure he'd give you a tour if you want."

"Of course, and your dad is his attorney."

"Yes," Heero shrugged. "It's time to grab something to eat. You should be hungry by now. While I was waiting, I placed an order of pasta bowls for the both of us. We can swing by and pick up our bibs for the race, and our dinner all in the same area."

"Afterwards, I'd like to go back to the hospital and be with my family."

"Would you like me to stay with you? I don't mind."

"Nah, you have things to do, and I think I want to be alone for a while with Gigi and my dad."

"You know if you need me. I'll be there. That's what *friends* are for." Heero gave me a fist bump.

"I do, thanks."

This time Heero put extra emphasis on *friends* and adding that fist bump let me know he wasn't expecting anything, even though we kissed earlier. Poor guy.

CHAPTER TEN

"Good morning, are you ready?" Heero asked before I could close the car door. "Have you eaten breakfast?

"Yep." My dad and I sat down for breakfast, before he left for the hospital. It's kind of our thing before games and any other events I compete in. He makes breakfast, we sit down together, and talk about what's coming up. And he gives me a pep talk. Always a pep talk. When I go away to college, I will miss his pep talks."

"That's a pretty cool ritual. So, what did he talk about?"

"You know, the regular coach Dad kind of stuff. Set a good pace. Watch my breathing and be mindful.

Most importantly enjoy the experience. Then he prayed for me, and you as well."

"Tell him thanks, I really appreciate that. Does that mean he won't be coming to the race?"

"No, he'll be there. He's going to the hospital first, then coming to the race. He wouldn't miss it. I told you, he's that parent that tries not to miss anything. He reschedules and shuffles his whole life to make sure he's there for me. He says we can't get back the special moments in life we miss. If he misses something, it's absolutely unavoidable."

"Cool. Are you ready?" Heero asked again. "You shouldn't be nervous."

"For the second time, I'm ready. You seem to be more nervous than I am. It looks like you're in need of a pep talk. Okay, listen. Take a deep breath. Come on do it with me. Take a deep breath. We've trained for this day. It's not your first race, just the first time you're running the full marathon. Treat it like any other race, and you will both do fine." I put my hand on his, resting on the gear shift.

"Thanks for the vote of confidence, and the pep talk. I needed that. To be honest, I can't help it. No matter how much I train, I still get nervous before a race. With this being my first full marathon, I'm more nervous than ever."

"Believe me, you will do just fine. Coach Pratt often tells us to trust the process. And right now, that's the best advice. You're asking me about eating, did you? You'll need to keep up your energy. You're race is much longer than mine."

"I ate what I could. When I say I'm nervous, I mean my stomach," Heero laughs. "I don't want to use the bathroom before the race. When I start running, I'll be able to settle down, and eventually feel better. In my pockets, I have sport beans, and Swedish fish for when I need something for energy."

Pulling up to the designated parking for race participants, I look around at all the cars and people. There are more people than I expected, and an awkward feeling is stirring in the pit of my stomach.

"You're starting to have the jitters," Heero laughs.

"A little," I shrug. But the sinking feeling in the pit of my stomach is not nerves about the race. "After today, we won't have a race to train for."

"You're right. And you don't have to see my mug if you don't want," Heero jokes.

I didn't think it was funny at all. The realization of all of our hard work coming to an end has me a little sad. No more basketball, or training for a race. What will I do with all the extra time? Will I need an excuse to see Heero? Thinking about it makes me unsettled.

"There are a lot of people here. I had no idea it would actually be this crowded." I look around in amazement as we walk into the race area to find our start corrals.

"It's a Boston Marathon qualifier, and people come from everywhere to participate in this race. Like thousands," Heero explains.

We stretch, and I can't stop looking and watching the droves of people pour in, stretching and getting prepared to race. There are young runners, my age and younger, older, as well as old-old runners possibly near Gigi and Pops age, give or take. They're all about to run the 10K, half and full marathon. I've never participated in an event with so many different age groups participating.

A whistle blows, and everyone starts to move. "That's the warning whistle. The race will start in ten minutes. It's time to go to our designated starting places. I'll see you at the finish line. Good luck."

We give each other fists bumps and Heero makes this weird face, making us both laugh.

"And good luck to you. I'll be waiting at the finish line," I said watching him walk away. That sinking feeling dropped lower in my stomach. I want to hug Heero, just to feel the spark of electricity that generates between the two of us. But I'm afraid to take anything from him. He'll need every bit of energy and focus he has for this race.

Feeling excited, nervous, and unsure all at the same time, I find my place in a crowd of others running the 10K. There is so much going, people are shuffling about, music blaring from speakers, and someone else talking into a microphone with a bullhorn. It's difficult to focus, and I remember what my dad said at the table while we were having breakfast. "If you find yourself getting overwhelmed, focus on your breathing and come back to center."

I'm doing just that, focusing on my breathing, centering myself, and tuning everyone else out. The air horn sounds, and the person with the bullhorn shouts, "Good luck! Good luck to you all."

Although the race starts, me and the others around me are standing still waiting our turn to start running. I breathe in and out focusing on the route I ran two days prior. I see myself running down Spring Street, and into the Bailey Quarters, imagining what the store fronts owned by Blacks looked like, like the Brantley Bakery, Williams Shoe Repair, and Aunt Neely's Place – Pop's said was the best dinner for home cooked meals. And if you didn't have any money, or just traveling through you could get a good meal and didn't have to worry about paying. Aunt Neely had a soft spot, and word was she would even feed stray cats and dogs in the alley. Because she was so generous paying customers always tipped heavy to help her provide for those in need and keep her place open.

"You gonna run, or you gonna stand here and daydream?" A lady slaps me on my butt, bringing me back to myself. "Let's go! See you at the finish line."

Starting the timekeeper on my smart watch, I begin slowly walking until I'm able to run. Weaving in and out of other runners and walkers I set my eyes on the butt slapper with the bobbing ponytail ahead of me and keep up with her pace. She's not fast at all, and she has more bounce to her run making it easy to spot her, which tickles me a little. Before long we're out of the crowds and passing mile marker one. My mind is clear, and I'm calm. So far so good.

At mile marker two, there is a water station. I'm good and keep running. But Ponytail slows down to grab a cup of water from one of the volunteers. "See you at the finish line," I wink at her and smile to myself. Coming into this race, I had no expectations. It's my very first, and I'm just here because of the rehab. But passing Ponytail has given me a goal. Stay in front of her and cross the finish line before she does, just became my mission. "I can do this," I say out loud to myself.

Shortly after passing the watering station at mile marker two, I wish I had taken a cup of water. I can use it right now, and I don't know when the next water station is coming up.

"Go, Nandi, go! Go, Nandi, go!" My dad is on the corner cheering for me. I slow down to wave and half pose for a picture.

"Photo bomb!" Ponytail yells as she passes me by. I don't have the extra energy to run by her. Instead, I coast in her wake and let her do all the work.

"Get the water, it's time you hydrate. We're about to hit a tough will, and you'll need it," Ponytail slows down long enough to tell me, and runs ahead.

I do just as she says and grab the cup at the next water station just past mile marker three. We didn't work on running and drinking. Note to self, something to work on. And just like she said we came to a hill, and a sign *you're halfway there.*

Keeping Ponytail in my view, I did what she did, walk some and run. Walk some and run. Walking up the hill at points allows me to preserve my energy. Challenging, but I conquer the hill and the route levels off. I have a burst of energy and will use it to run past Ponytail when I catch her slacking. My intentions are to put enough distance between us so I can stay ahead of her. Much like Coach Pratts strategy during a basketball game, put more points on the board than our opponent, and then pull away from them.

The end has to be close; the halfway point seems so long ago. and I'm struggling. Walking more often just trying to stay in the race, I look over my shoulder to see where Ponytail is. For good measure I pick up the pace of my walk to a very slow jog.

"I'm back here," a voice laughs. "This is the time you pick up your speed and run ahead of me."

I don't have the energy to speed up, and Ponytail has run past me and on out of sight. Instead, of focusing on losing to an older lady, older than my mom, but not as old as Gigi beating me, I focus on finishing strong. My thoughts go to Heero. I wonder how he's doing. Where he is in the race, if he's struggling, and if there is anyone pushing him to his best.

From wondering about Heero, my mind shifts to what will I do without our training sessions. We've just started working out and hanging out again. I'm not ready for *this*, whatever *this* is between me and Heero to end. Right now, in a moment of extreme fatigue, I come to a full understanding, Heero is more than my friend. I'm not willing to let go of what we have.

"Looking good Nandi!"

"Way to go! You've got this!"

"You've got this! Go Nandi, go!"

It's my teammates. They're cheering, waving signs, and giving me the last push, I need to finish the race. The finish line is one hundred yards away. With the biggest smile on my face, I suck it up, and sprint the rest of the way in.

"I got you. I got you." Ponytail meets me at the finish line just in time to catch me before I fall to the ground. "Come on, just lean on me and lets walk it out. You can't stop abruptly, or you'll cramp up really bad."

"Thank you. Thank you so much," I pant, as she puts a sports drink in my hand.

"No, thank you. You pushed me to my personal best time ever. And I owe you big time. Was this your first 10K?" she asks.

"Yes," was all I could get out, along with a nod, while still catching my breath and trying not to guzzle the sports drink.

"You did really good. I am impressed with your athleticism, and hope this is not your last 10K. My friends call me Pinky, I own a bookstore and gift shop, *The Book Ends* in Harbor Springs. When you're out that way, stop in and say hi. Here comes a happy bunch, I think they're waiting to congratulate you."

"We are so proud of you!" Emily squeals, and the rest of the girls huddle around me for a group hug, and chant.

"I am so excited to see you guys. Your cheers gave me the push I needed at the end to make it across the finish line. 'Cause a sister was spent!"

"You didn't look tired at all Nandi. Are you sure this was your first race? Your form and ease said you've done this before," Pixie adds her two cents.

"Thanks for saying so, but I know you're lying," I laugh. "My tongue was just about to drag the ground."

CHAPTER ELEVEN

Recovering from the race, I'm setting up my wait and watch station. Yesterday, I took everything to Emily I need for post-race. A sports chair, umbrella, cooler with drinks and snacks, along with the signs for Heero's finish line celebration. She brought them out for me when the team came to cheer me on.

"It's going to be another couple of hours," a race official says walking along the race barrier. "If there is something you want to do, there is time to get it done, and come back before the first runners start coming in."

"Thanks, but I'll be waiting right here," I tell him, pulling out a sandwich from the cooler. Just my luck,

I move for anything, and that will be the time Heero comes in and I miss him.

"Suit yourself."

Smiling to myself, I feel accomplished after running my very first 10K, whether it's my last or not, is still up for debate. I almost forgot about the app and tracking Heero's progress. He helped me set it up a couple days ago. At three hours into the race Heero has passed the fifteen-mile mark and seem to have a pretty good pace.

"Go, Heero. Go!" I chant out loud.

"I didn't think I'd be able to find you. Wow, you've got a serious set up," Heero's brother laughed.

"Hey, Tayo. You shouldn't go around sneaking up on people," I laugh with him.

"I'm sorry. Do you have any idea where he might be?"

"I do. According to this app, a few minutes ago, Heero was passing the fifteen-mile mark. By my calculations it should be a little more than an hour or so before he crosses the finish line. Is anyone else from your family coming out to support him?"

"Not today, our parents are busy, and granddad, sends his regards via cash."

"I don't have another chair, but you're welcome to sit on my cooler, it's pretty sturdy."

"I'll just take a seat here on the ground next to you. Thanks."

We sit in silence watching race officials move around like busy ants. I've only met Tayo a hand full of times, and I'm the worst at small talk. And with someone I don't know, it's like pulling teeth from a shark. Instead of trying to force any conversation, I eat. The race took a lot out of me, and I am starving.

"Heero says you're a pretty good baller," Tayo says.

"I do okay."

"Okay, huh. You also have Mr. Harshaw singing your praise to our parents. I'd say you're more than okay."

"Is that so?" Now I'm intrigued. Mr. Harshaw talking to Heero's parents about me I feel uncovered, and naked. "He's really nice, and he stuck his neck out for me. My family and I are appreciative."

"As you should be. Mr. Harshaw is nice, but he's also a shrewd businessman who has an eye for potential and great talent. His backing you, and talking you up, says a lot about you. And heads up. You're now on my parents; radar, especially my mom's."

I start feeling somewhat nervous, almost uncomfortable. It seems as if Tayo is feeling me out to see if I am who and what Mr. Harshaw says I am. And what in the hell does he mean by I'm on his parents radar? One thing I know for certain, Mrs. Ibeh is not happy that Heero and I have been spending so much time together. My parents are not doctors, lawyers, or of any profession that meets her particular standards.

The very first time I met Mrs. Ibeh, Heero and I went by his house before a training session because he didn't get his bag that morning before leaving for school. He left me in the kitchen eating a snack, while he ran upstairs to change his clothes. In the time he was gone, I got the third degree from his mom.

"Good afternoon, I am Heero's mom, Judge Ibeh. Who are your parents?" Were the first things she said to me. Next, she asked if I had been a debutante, or been asked to be a part of the local cotillion.

When I told her who my parents are, and that I had not been in a cotillion, she sucked her teeth and left me in the kitchen alone. I knew that was not a good thing. And now to hear I'm on her radar, it almost has me shaking in my boots.

Cheers and yells from the crowd start as the first few runners appear in the distance about a quarter of a mile out. Tayo and I stand and join in the cheering, and I check to see if it's Heero. It's not.

"How did you do in the 10K? It was the 10K you ran this morning, right?" Tayo asks. He is visibly getting impatient with waiting.

"Yes, I did run the 10K. Let me guess, Heero told you that as well?" I laugh. "For my very first 10K, I think I did pretty good. My time was eighty minutes."

"Will you be running another race anytime soon?"

"I don't know just yet. This one was a means of doing extra to help me strengthen my leg and get me back to basketball."

"I see. When Heero got into running, he didn't plan on continuing to run either. After his first race, he was hooked. He's run a few 10K's, then it wasn't long before he was running half marathons. He's addicted. Watch out, you'll be addicted too."

"Nah, basketball is my sport."

"Okay. Remember I warned you."

"Do you play any sports?" I ask. Not making small talk necessarily, I genuinely want to know.

"Our older brother Ibrahim and I were not allowed to play sports. We had to focus on our education. It was decided for us, that we would be lawyers and to attend our parents Alma Mater. And to do so it was necessary that we commit to academics. But when Heero came along, he was allowed more freedoms. He possessed natural athletic abilities as a small child. Mother took that as a sign that he might not be as smart as everyone else and let him find his way. Ibrahim has always been jealous of Heero's freedoms, but I've lived through him and enjoyed watching him thrive at everything he's tried, so effortlessly."

I am shocked that Tayo is opening up to me in this way.

"Here comes another pack!" someone yells, as the cheers start again to welcome the runners to the finish line.

"Is it Heero?" Tayo asks. "I can't tell, and I don't know what color he was wearing."

"Nah, it's not him," I continue cheering for the runners approaching the finish line. "He's wearing blue. We're actually matching."

"Isn't that cute, the two of you are Twinkies. Can you check to see where he is now? There is a steady stream of runners coming in, he should be coming in soon." Tayo asks.

"It shows him around the twenty-two-mile mark. But it looks like he's either stopped or he's going very slow. Hold on let me refresh."

"Twenty-two. That's a little more than four miles left to go. Why would he stop?" Tayo questioned.

"I don't know, and the app has him barely moving. I'll be back," I tell Tayo before thinking twice.

"You'll be back. What am I supposed to do with your stuff?"

"Whatever you want!" I yell, making my way through the crowd along the barricade. My only thought is getting to Heero and soon as right now.

I'm not getting anywhere through the crowd of people, so I cross over the barricade and run on the sidelines. A race official and I make eye contact. It looks as if she wanted to say something. I point, she nods, and I keep it moving. At this point, I'm running full out.

"Hey. You're running in the wrong direction!" a spectator hollers from behind the barricade.

"Thanks for that!" I yell back, and stop to take a breather and check the app. It now shows Heero at mile twenty-three, and I feel like I've run about two miles. I'm close. Grabbing a cup of water from a water station, I jog, looking through the crowds of runners. I spot Heero at a distance. My heart and emotions tell me to run to him. But my head says wait.

I watch Heero jog several yards, grimacing and

then stop and hold the back of his leg. It's his hamstring. He's attempts to jog again and stop to walk. Pain and agony is all over his face, as well as in the limp of his walk and jog. Runners are passing him by. I feel for him, but I also know he is very proud. Instead of stopping, Heero is determined to finish.

In an attempt to jog again, Heero looks up to see me waiting. He shrugs and smiles, almost relieved to see me. I jog over to him, and slide under his arm. "Lean on me, I'll help you finish," I tell him. With around three miles to go, Heero uses me as support, and tries to walk, more like a hobble, as fast as he could. We got into a rhythm. More runners were passing us, and a man with a disability, who jogs sideways passes us. Before long, the blue lights of the police escort are behind us.

Heero blows, in frustration.

"Don't mind any of that, only concentrate on finishing. Finishing is all that matters," I tell him.

"Thank you," Heero whispers. "Thank you for being here for me."

"What are your expectations?" I ask as we keep up our pace.

"Excuse me?" Heero looks at me.

"Your expectations. You once asked me about my expectations, why am I working out and training?

Now I'm asking you, what is your end goal, or are you just going through the motions for the fun of it? Are you only in it for the fun? If so, that's okay too. When we started working out together, we were not on the same page. But today I'm sure that we are. We're both doing something we've never done, to obtain a goal we've never reached. And along the way we've taken a few risks. Do you remember that?"

"You pick a helluva time to remind me of what I said," Heero smiled through his pain, and stopped hobbling to catch his breath. "Yes, I remember saying that. But can we finish this race?"

"There is something I need you to know before we go one step further. I'm serious about us, it's not something I'm doing to pass the time, and I'm not wasting your time. You don't have to say anything or react." I look away, nervous about what I would see in his eyes.

We are a quarter mile from the finish line, and many of the spectators are gone. The few that are left along with Tayo are cheering for Heero, and he smiles.

"Finish strong," Heero says pulling away from me. "I've got this."

"Finish strong," I repeat and run ahead to join

Tayo on the sidelines to cheer Heero across the finish line with my sign, and noise maker.

"You found him!" Tayo said surprised.

"Of course, I did."

CHAPTER TWELVE

Watching Heero struggle, and limping trying to make it to the finish line, my heart goes out to him. But I also knew if he struggles this hard for something he wants, like this race, then I can count on him to fight for us.

Cheering loud and hard from my gut in an effort to help Heero across the finish line. Laughing to myself, the way I am cheering reminds me of my mom. When I was like third grade playing youth league basketball, one game we were getting beat so bad, and so far behind in points the officials just let the clock run. The mercy rule. We were making more bricks than baskets. At that time, I was still learning how to play the game, and wasn't very good. But my mom cheered like we were national champions. As much as I tell myself I don't miss her being in the stands and being my fan, today, I do.

Tayo starts with a low "Go, Heero go! Go, Heero go!"

The few people left in the crowd join in until it's a loud roar. "Go, Heero go! Go, Heero go!" encouraging him to make those last few steps and cross the finish line.

Almost there, Heero goes down, and the crowd stops chanting. You can literally hear us holding our collective breaths willing Heero to get up.

"Give him a minute." I catch Tayo by the arm attempting to run out to help his younger brother.

Struggling, Heero is able to get back to his feet, and the crowd cheers harder and louder, as he makes it over the finish line collapsing into Tayo's arms. I pull the string, and red, white, and silver confetti falls in seemingly slow motion. Heero's too exhausted to even notice it. He keeps repeating "Finish strong. Finish strong."

Under Heero's arms, Tayo and I walk him to the medical tent for assistance and hydration.

"You did it," I tell Heero, handing him a sports drink and gel. "Drink and eat these. You need to replenish electrolytes."

"All I need is you." Heero sits up on the table, pulling me to himself. "I may have been in pain out there and misunderstood what you said. Right here and right now, I need clarity."

"There will be time for that later. You should hydrate and let them wrap your hamstring," I tell him trying to back away from the table.

Heero holds on to me, looks into my eyes. "Tell me if I recall correctly, you said you're serious about us, it's not something you're doing to pass the time, or waste mine."

"Yes. You understand perfectly." I hold his face in my hands. Never have I been surer of anything than I am at this moment. This time my heart, my head, and my emotions aren't betraying me. I'm no longer suppressing the feelings I have for Heero into the deepest parts of me. I know for sure what I'm feeling for Heero, and it's all real.

Unlike the first time we kissed, I am fully aware and intentional about what I am doing. With his face in my hands, I gently kiss Heero again and again.

"Ow, ow, ow!" Heero groans.

"Did I hurt you?" I step back concerned.

"Yes, and do it again," Heero laughs, grabbing my hands and pulling me into him.

We kiss and laugh making it difficult for the

medics to work on his leg. Just like spring inevitably turns into summer, our nothing is the start of something.

The End

THE START OF
SOMETHING?
the inevitable book two
L.M.
RICHARDSON

"I have a great idea," Heero walks through the door smiling, greeting me with a kiss.

Since the marathon and graduation Heero and I have been together more than we're apart. As soon as we get off work we're together until late into the night. A couple of times he's literally spent the night. We fell asleep watching movies and woke up on the couch about five in the morning, the newspaper was on the front porch. And he'd sneak into his house, before anyone realized he wasn't home.

And when we're not with each other, we're on the phone. Talking like we had not seen each other for weeks.

Emily says it's the novelty of our relationship, and we're still in the honeymoon phase where we're eating each other up. She promises it will end. I hope she's wrong because I am enjoying everything about Heero. He makes me smile, and as hard as I try not to be giddy around him, it's an epic fail.

"I hope your good idea doesn't involve making collages with those magazines and pamphlets you're waving in my face. Collage making was not a strong point for me in elementary school. More glue and magazine pages ended up stuck to my clothes than to the paper."

"You read my mind, grab your scissors. Just kidding," Heero hugs me tight, dipping and kissing me 'til I laugh and snort. "There's that laugh I love. Seriously, these are not for cutting and pasting. I picked them up from the Convention and Visitors Bureau. Did you know there are so many fun and interesting things to see in do right here in Caledonia? Some I knew about, and many I didn't."

"Go ahead, you have my attention."

"Things we can see and do together, to make memories and get to know each other better," Heero said with the biggest smile, and proud of himself. "We have nine weeks of summer together before we leave for college. And I don't want to waste a day of it."

"That's so…"

"Damn mushy." Gigi laughs coming into the room. "I'm just kidding. Young love is enchanting in all its naivete, and the two of you are beautifully ignorant. I hope you're able to stay that way for a very long time."

"Was that meant to be a compliment?" Heero questioned.

"Indeed, it was," Gigi confirms.

"Thanks, I guess." Heero laughs.

"Well, I think it's nice and romantic," I smile at Heero with approval. "Let me see those magazines and pamphlets, and let's get started planning a summer to remember. What do you have in mind?"

"I was worried you'd think it was a dumb idea. Most of these places are within an hour's drive, and we can come up with a few other ideas outside of these." Heero returns the smile. "With both of us going to different colleges, making our summer together special is important to me. My personal favorites are the state parks, but I'm not sure about how you feel about being outside in nature with bugs, and all."

"Being outside is cool, and I'm even okay with bugs, as long as you're not trying to put any in my shirt. Green Peaks mountain," I said grabbing one of the pamphlets. "I've wanted to hike this mountain since about sixth grade. Before Pops got sick, he said he would take me hiking there to see this really cool waterfall. This one is an absolute must!"

"Of course," Heero agrees. "And what do you think about canoeing? I've only done it twice with my boy scout troop, but I think it will be great to do together."

"Swimming is not on my list of proficiencies, and I've never been in a canoe, but I'm willing to try new things. And what better time than now, with my guy to do them?"

"This is going to be the best summer ever. What do you say we get started now?" Heero gets up from the table and grabs my hand as if we're about to dance.

"Right now?" I laugh.

"Yes, right now. There's no better time than the present. Isn't that how the saying goes? This *Popup in the Park*, an arts and crafts festival in Millwood Park is happing now through the rest of the weekend," Heero said, picking up one of the pamphlets. "It's next to the farmers market. It should be a lot of fun."

"Now is perfect! This event will definitely be a first for me. I'd love to hit up the farmer's market while we're there. Ms. Margret grows and sells *the* best strawberries I've ever eaten. The sweetest, just like candy. Once you have hers, you'll never want them from anywhere else. I haven't had them in a couple of years, but I'm told she still sells there. Just let me grab my bag, and a pair of shoes."

"There's someone at the door for you!" Heero hollers as soon as I get to the other room.

"Who is it? Ask them what they want?"

"Ummm. She says she's your mom."

"Quit playing. I told you about my mom. She's not coming back." I said, walking to the door to find Gigi, Heero, and my mom all standing there watching for my reaction.

My mom is actually standing in the door of Gigi's house, with her bags. Although it's been ten years, she doesn't seem to have aged or changed much except for her hair. It's longer and looks to be natural.

"You ready?" I ask Heero walking out of the door past her.

"Nandi?" I heard Gigi calling.

"Are you not going to…" Heero starts to ask, getting in the car.

"Can we just go? I'd rather not deal with her, and the nerve she has to show up, out of nowhere."

THE START OF NOTHING

the inevitable series book one

L.M. RICHARDSON

Thank you for being the best part of my journey!